SHAKESPEARE FOR YOUNG PEOPLE

A Midsummer Night's Dream

ROMEO AND JULIET

Titania: I love thee!

SHAKESPEARE FOR YOUNG PEOPLE

A MIDSUMMER NIGHT'S DREAM

by
William Shakespeare

edited and illustrated by
Diane Davidson

SWAN BOOKS
A division of Learning Links Inc.
New Hyde Park, New York

Published by:

SWAN BOOKS
a division of
LEARNING LINKS INC.
2300 Marcus Avenue
New Hyde Park, NY 11042

Copyright © 2000, 2002
by Learning Links Inc.

Originally Published by
Marie Diane Davidson
Copyright © 1986

Permission to use the music of
"Over Hill, Over Dale" by Sandy Harrison
(© 1986 by Warren Harrison)
has been arranged through courtesy of
the late composer's estate.

Printed in the United States of America

Library of Congress Cataloging-in-Publication Data

Shakespeare, William 1564-1616.
    A Midsummer Night's Dream for young people.

    (Shakespeare for young people)
    Summary : An abridged version of Shakespeare's
original text with a character as an "announcer" who
summarizes deleted passages. Includes some staging
directions.
    ISBN 0-7675-0835-1
    1. Children's plays, English. [1. Plays]
I. Davidson, Diane. II. Harrison, Sandy. III. Title.
IV. Series: Shakespeare, William, 1564-1616.
Shakespeare for young people
PR2827.A25 1986   822.3'3   86-5957

TO THE TEACHER OR PARENT

Young people can grow up loving Shakespeare if they act out his plays. Since Shakespeare wrote for the theater, not for the printed page, he is most exciting on his own ground.

Many people are afraid that the young will not understand Shakespeare's words. To help these actors follow the story, the editor has added two optional announcers, who introduce and explain scenes. However, young people pick up the general meaning with surprising ease, and they enjoy the words without completely understanding them at first. Their ears tell them the phrases often sound like music, and the plays are full of marvelous scenes.

After all, Shakespeare is not called the best of all writers because he is hard. He is the best of all writers because he is enjoyable!

HOW TO BEGIN

At first, students may find the script too difficult to enjoy, so one way to start is for the director to read the play aloud. Between scenes, he can ask, "What do you think is going to happen next?" or "Do you think the characters should do this?" After the students become familiar with the story and words, they can try out for parts by reading different scenes. In the end, the director should pick the actors he thinks are best, emphasizing, "There are no small parts. Everybody helps in a production."

The plays can be presented in several ways.

In the simplest form, the students can read the script aloud, sitting in their seats. This will do well enough, but it is more fun to put on the actual show.

What can a director do to help his actors?

One main point in directing is to have the actors speak the words loudly and clearly. It helps if they speak a little

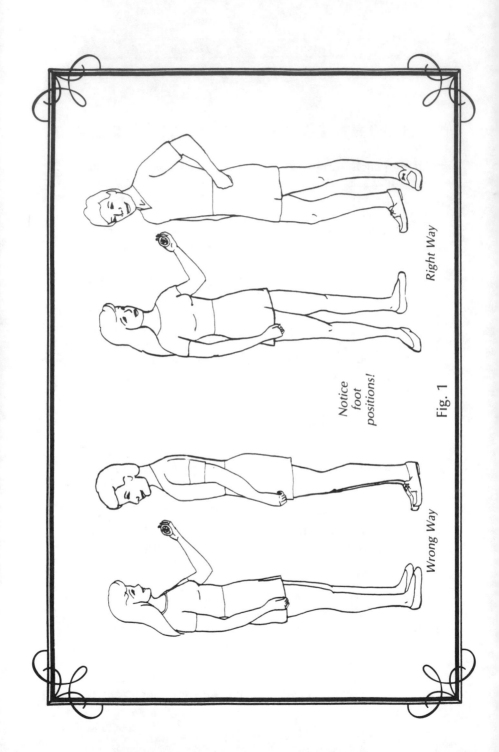

Wrong Way

Right Way

Notice
foot
positions!

Fig. 1

more slowly than usual. They should not be afraid to pause or to emphasize short phrases. However, they should not try to be "arty" or stilted. Shakespeare wrote very energetic plays.

A second main point in directing is to keep the students facing the audience, even if they are talking to someone else. They should "fake front," so that their bodies face the audience and their heads are only half-way towards the other actors. (Fig. 1)

The cast should be told that when the announcers speak between scenes, servants can continue to change the stage set, and actors can enter, exit, or stand around pretending to talk silently. But if an announcer speaks during a scene, the actors should "freeze" until the announcer has finished his lines. At no time should the actors look at the announcers. (The announcers' parts may be cut out if the director so desires.)

Encouragement and applause inspire the young to do better, and criticism should always be linked with a compliment. Often, letting the students find their own way through the play produces the best results. And telling them, "Mean what you say," or "Be more energetic!" is all they really need.

SCHEDULES AND BUDGET

Forty-five minutes a day—using half the time for group scenes and half the time for individual scenes—is generally enough for students to rehearse. The director should encourage all to learn their lines as soon as possible. An easy way to memorize lines is to tape them and have the student listen to the tape at home each evening, going over it four or five times. Usually actors learn faster by ear than by eye. In all, it takes about six weeks to prepare a good show.

The play seems more complete if it has an audience, even other people from next door. But an afternoon or evening public performance is better yet. A PTA meeting, Open House, a Renaissance Fair, a holiday—all are excellent times to do a play.

To attract a good crowd, the admission should be very small or free. However, a Drama Fund is always useful, so some groups pass a hat, or parents sell cookies and punch. But the best way to raise money for a Drama Fund is to sell advertising in the program. A business-card size ad can sell for $5 to $10, and a larger ad brings in even more. This money can be used for costumes or 250-500 watt spotlights. Until there is money in the Drama Fund, the director often becomes an expert at borrowing and improvising. Fortunately, Shakespeare's plays can be produced with almost no scenery, and there are no royalties to pay.

SPECIAL NOTES ON THIS PLAY

A Midsummer Night's Dream needs only simple staging: two "wings" or screens on each side of the playing area. If the school has a stage, fine. But good shows can take place at one end of a room.

What can people use as screens? Tall cardboard refrigerator boxes are good. Stage flats, frames of 1" x 4" lumber joined by triangles of plywood and covered with muslin sheeting, are excellent, if little side flats are hinged to the main one, to provide bracing.

In *A Midsummer Night's Dream*, there are basically two scenes: Athens and the magic wood. If two pieces of cloth or cardboard are painted as a Greek pillar with clouds on one side and a tree on the other, then hung on the back wall, the group has all the scenery needed. When the setting changes, two actors can simply turn the pictures around. (Fig. 2)

The director should decide one side of the stage is the direction of Athens and the other side the magic wood.

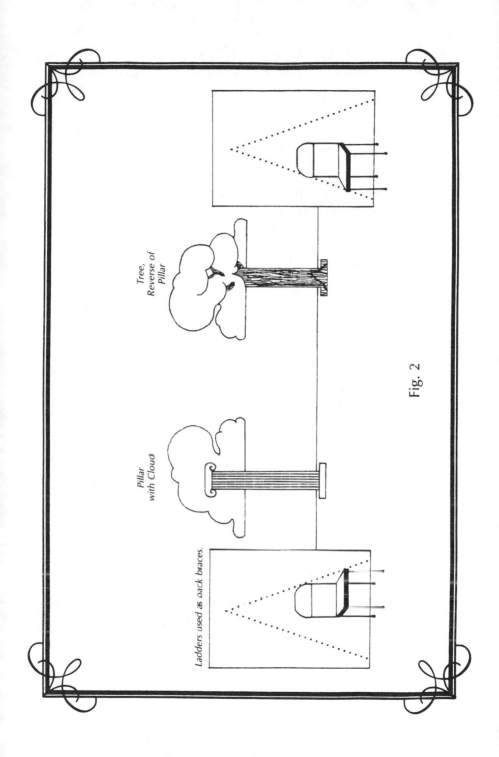

Ladders used as back braces.

Pillar
with Cloud

Tree,
Reverse of
Pillar

Fig. 2

On each side of the stage should be chairs where the two announcers sit during scenes.

A Midsummer Night's Dream takes Greek costumes for people of the Duke's court, very simple tunics with a cord around the waist. To help the audience understand the plot, it is best to have Lysander and Hermia with the same colored trim on their tunics (for instance, blue) while Demetrius and Helena have another color (yellow, perhaps). The workmen can wear dark shirts and pants, the legs tied criss-cross with string. And the fairy folk can be as fantastic as desired, with scarves and streamers of crepe paper and head-bands with antennae. Oberon should have a cloak that he draws across his face to become invisible.

The major prop is the donkey head for Bottom. This can be rented, but it is simpler to make one. (Fig. 3)

An easy costume for Lion can be made by tying a grass hula skirt (or a crepe paper copy of one) around Lion's head, bandana fashion, so it forms the mane. Add a cat makeup with black nose, split upper lip, and whiskers. The rest of the costume can be Snug's ordinary clothing.

A word of warning is necessary: though the actors have swords, no one really fights, and the students should be very careful not to play with even imitation swords, as someone may be hurt.

For background music, no one could make a better choice than Elizabethan music or Mendelssohn's *A Midsummer Night's Dream.*

A LAST BIT OF ADVICE

How will a director know if he has produced Shakespeare "correctly"? He can ask his group if they had fun. If they answer, "Yes," then the show is a success!

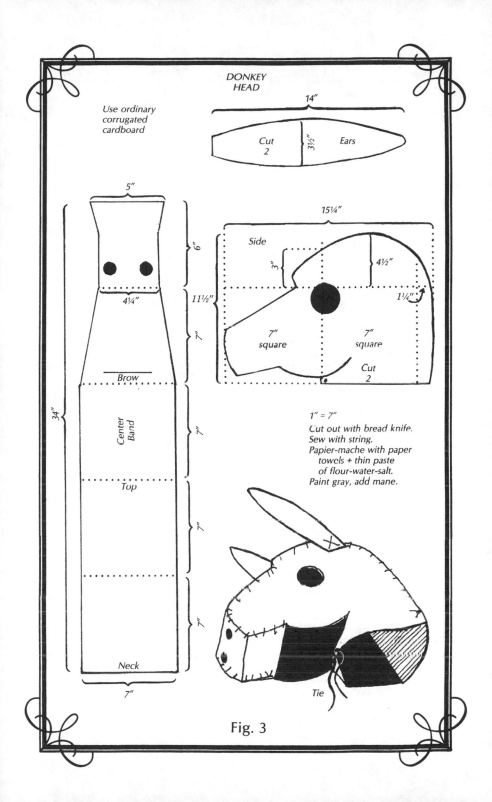

DONKEY HEAD

Use ordinary corrugated cardboard

14"

Cut 2   3½"   Ears

5"

6"

4¼"

11½"

7"

Brow

Center Band

Top

Neck

34"

7"

7"

7"

7"

15¼"

Side

3"

4½"

1¼"

7" square   7" square

Cut 2

1" = 7"

Cut out with bread knife.
Sew with string.
Papier-mache with paper towels + thin paste of flour-water-salt.
Paint gray, add mane.

Tie

Fig. 3

CHARACTERS

Two Announcers (optional), who have been added.

At the Duke's Court
Theseus (**Thee**-see-us), the noble Duke of Athens
Hippolyta (Hip-**pol**-uh-tuh), Queen of the Amazons, Theseus' bride-to-be
Egeus (Ee-**gee**-us), Hermia's harsh father
Lysander (Lie-**san**-der), Hermia's loving sweetheart
Demetrius (Dee-**mee**-tree-us) Hermia's demanding admirer
Hermia (**Her**-mee-uh), engaged to Loving Lysander
Helena, in love with Demanding Demetrius
Philostrate (**Phil**-oh-strate), the Master of Revels or Master of Ceremonies for the court
Ladies and Gentlemen

In a Workman's Cottage
Peter Quince, the old director of the amateur play
Nick Bottom, a weaver and ham actor who plays heroes
Snug, a stupid furniture-maker who plays the lion
Flute, a bellows-mender who has to play the heroine
Snout, a tinker who plays a wall
Starveling, a tailor who plays the moon

In the Land of Faerie
    Oberon (**Oh**-ber-on), the proud King of the Fairies
    Titania (Ti-**tan**-ee-uh), the lovely Fairy Queen
    Puck, a mischievous little goblin
    Peaseblossom, Cobweb, Moth, Mustardseed—
        young fairies
    Elves and Fairies

ACT I

(A couple of Greek pillars indicate the scenery. Two announcers enter, bow and take their places on each side of the stage area.)

Announcer 1: (To the audience) Welcome, everyone, to a production of Shakespeare's *A Midsummer Night's Dream* given by the _____ class. ·

Announcer 2: This is not the complete play but a very short edition for young people, using the original words.

Announcer 1: We two announcers have been added to the play to help explain any hard parts.

Announcer 2: You will notice some long words, because in Shakespeare's time people played with words, like a game with sounds.

Announcer 1: The story begins in Ancient Athens, in the time of Greek heroes. One of the heroes was Theseus, Duke of Athens.

Announcer 2: Theseus was at war with Hippolyta, the Queen of the Amazons.

(Theseus and Hippolyta come to the center of the stage, their swords in their hands. They cross their swords, ready to fight.)

Announcer 1: However, they fell in love and decided it would be more fun to get married.

(Theseus and Hippolyta put their swords in their belts. She holds out her hand to him and smiles, as he kneels and kisses it.)

Announcer 2: Now Duke Theseus plans a big celebration. *(The announcers sit quietly and watch.)*

Theseus: (Rising from his knees) Hippolyta, I wooed thee with my sword. But I will wed thee in another key—with pomp, with triumph and with reveling!

Annnouncer 1: However, his happy plans are interrupted by an angry father, Egeus.

(Cross old Egeus hobbles in with his pretty little daughter Hermia. She is followed by two young men: her Loving Lysander and Demanding Demetrius.)

Egeus: (Bowing) Happy be Theseus, our Duke!

Theseus: Thanks, good Egeus. What's the news with thee?

Egeus: (Angrily) Full of vexation come I, with complaint against my daughter Hermia. *(Hermia curtsies.)*

Announcer 2: Hermia refuses to marry the man her father has chosen. She wants to marry the man she loves.

Egeus: (Motioning to one of the young men.) Stand forth, Demetrius. *(Demetrius bows to the Duke.)* My noble lord, this man hath my consent to marry her. *(Egeus motions to the other young man.)* Stand forth, Lysander. *(Lysander bows and waves to Hermia. She giggles and waves back. Her father frowns.)* And, my gracious Duke, this hath bewitched my child. *(Angrily)* Thou, thou, Lysander, thou hast by moonlight at her window sung! With cunning hast thou filched my daughter's heart!

Announcer 1: According to law, Egeus can have Hermia killed if she disobeys him.

Egeus: (To the Duke) And, my gracious Duke, I beg, as she is mine, I may dispose of her to this gentleman . . . *(He points to Demetrius.)* . . . or to her death, according to our law! *(All look horrified.)*

Theseus: What say you, Hermia? Demetrius is a worthy gentleman.

Hermia: (In tears) So is Lysander! *(She steps forward and kneels.)* Pardon me, but I beseech your Grace that I may know the worst if I refuse to wed Demetrius.

(For a moment Theseus and his Queen whisper.)

Announcer 2: The Duke decides to give Hermia one more choice if she does not marry Demetrius: she can become a nun in a temple of Diana, the goddess of the moon.

Theseus: (To Hermia) Either to die the death or to endure the livery of a nun, chanting faint hymns to the cold fruitless moon.

Hermia: (Rising, determined to be a nun.) So I will live, so die, my lord!

Demetrius: (Wanting her to change.) Relent, sweet Hermia!

Lysander: You have her father's love, Demetrius. Let me have Hermia's. *(He laughs.)* Do you marry **him**!

Egeus: Scornful Lysander!

Announcer 1: Besides, Demetrius has already broken the heart of another girl, Helena.

Lysander: (Kneeling before the Duke.) My lord, my love is more than his ... *(He points at Demetrius.)* ... and I am beloved of beauteous Hermia! *(With scorn)* Demetrius made love to Nedar's daughter, Helena, and won her soul!

Theseus: (Worried) I must confess that I have heard so much. But Demetrius, come. And come, Egeus. *(To the girl)* For you, fair Hermia, look you fit your fancies to your father's will, or else the law of Athens yields you up—to death, or to a vow of single life!

(The Duke and the Queen, followed by Egeus and Demetrius, leave in the direction of Athens. When they are alone, Hermia cries on Lysander's shoulder. He speaks to her gently.)

Lysander: How now, my love? The course of true love never did run smooth. So quick bright things come to confusion.

Hermia: (Sadly) Then let us teach our trial patience.

Announcer 2: But Lysander has a plan—to elope to his aunt's house and get married there.

Lysander: (Smiling) Hear me, Hermia. I have a widow aunt. From Athens is her house . . . *(He points away.)* . . . seven leagues. She respects me as her only son. There, gentle Hermia, may I marry thee!

Announcer 1: They can meet in the forest just outside of Athens, the next night.

Lysander: (As Hermia smiles through her tears.) If thou lovest me then, steal forth thy father's house tomorrow night. And in the wood without the town, there will I stay for thee!

Hermia: Tomorrow truly will I meet with thee!

Announcer 2: But in comes Helena, Demetrius's former sweetheart. And she will really cause trouble.

(Helena, a tall blonde, comes running in, mopping her tears with a handkerchief.)

Hermia: God speed, fair Helena!

Helena: (Sniffling) Call you me "fair"? Demetrius loves **your** "fair." O happy fair! *(She wails loudly.)*

Hermia: I frown upon him, yet he loves me still.

Helena: Oh, that your frowns would teach my smiles such skill!

Hermia: The more I hate, the more he follows me.

Helena: The more I love, the more he hateth me!

Hermia: Take comfort! He no more shall see my face. *(She smiles to see Helena stop crying and listen.)*

Lysander: Helena, tomorrow night, through Athens' gates have we devised to steal . . .

Hermia: . . . and in the wood, there my Lysander and myself shall meet. And then from Athens turn away our eyes, to seek new friends. *(She kisses Helena gently.)* Farewell, sweet playfellow. And good luck grant thee thy Demetrius! *(Hermia and Lysander leave in the direction of the wood.)*

Helena: (To herself, sadly) How happy some can be! Through Athens I am thought as fair as she. But what of that? Demetrius thinks not so. *(Suddenly she has an idea.)* I will go tell him of fair Hermia's flight! Then to the wood will he tomorrow night pursue her. And for this, if I have thanks, it is a dear expense! *(She leaves in the direction of Athens.)*

Announcer 1: While Helena goes to tell Demetrius of the runaway lovers, a group of workingmen of Athens gather together.

Announcer 2: They want to put on a little play to entertain the Duke after the wedding. Now they are meeting to rehearse.

(Old Peter Quince enters with a number of playscripts. The amateur actors follow him: loud Bottom, stupid Snug, squeaky Flute, practical Snout,

and timid Starveling. Quince looks at them over his spectacles.)

Quince: Is all our company here?

Bottom: (In a big, jolly voice.) You were best to call them man by man.

Quince: (Looking at a list) Here is the scroll of every man's name, which is thought fit to play before the Duke and the Duchess on his wedding day at night.

Bottom: First, good Peter Quince, say what the play treats on.

Quince: (Reading the title with pride.) Marry, our play is "The Most Lamentable Comedy and Most Cruel Death of Pyramus and Thisby."

Bottom: (Clapping his hands) A very good piece of work! *(To the others)* Masters, spread yourselves. *(All the actors sit on the floor.)*

Quince: Answer as I call you. Nick Bottom, the weaver!

Bottom: (Standing at attention) Ready! Name what part I am for!

Quince: You, Nick Bottom, are set down for Pyramus.

Bottom: (Eagerly) What is Pryramus? A lover or a tyrant?

Quince: A lover that kills himself, most gallant, for love!

Bottom: (He slaps his chest and waves his arms as he boasts.) That will ask some tears in the true performing of it. If I do it, let the audience look to their eyes. I will move storms! *(All applaud him.)* Now name the rest of the players.

Quince: (Peering at his list again.) Francis Flute, the bellows-mender.

Flute: (Squeaking) Here, Peter Quince!

Quince: You must take Thisby on you.

Flute: What is Thisby? *(He smiles brightly.)* A wandering knight?

Quince: It is the lady that Pyramus must love.

Flute: (Horrified) Nay, faith, let not me play a woman! *(He rubs his chin.)* I have a beard coming!

Quince: (Firmly) That's all one. You may speak as small as you will.

Bottom: (Wanting to take every part.) Let **me** play Thisby too. I'll speak in a monstrous little voice. *(He speaks in a shrill woman's voice.)* "Ah, Pyramus, my lover dear! Thy Thisby dear, and lady dear!" *(He flutters his eyelashes, and the others applaud.)*

Quince: (Irritated) No, no! You must play Pyramus. And, Flute, you Thisby.

Bottom: (Disappointed) Well, proceed. *(He sits down.)*

Quince: Robin Starveling, the tailor!

Starveling: (Shyly) Here, Peter Quince.

Quince: Robin Starveling, you must play Thisby's mother. Tom Snout, the tinker!

Snout: (Solidly) Here, Peter Quince!

Quince: You, Pyramus' father. Myself, Thisby's father. Snug the joiner—you, the lion's part. *(He smiles at all broadly.)* And I hope here is a play fitted.

Snug: (Very stupid) Have you the lion's part written? Pray you, give it me, for I am slow of study.

Quince: It is nothing but roaring.

Bottom: (With an excited leap to his feet.) Let **me** play the lion too! I will roar that I will do any man's heart good to hear me. *(He growls and roars loudly.)* I will roar, that I will make the Duke say, "Let him roar again! Let him roar again!"

Quince: (With disapproval) You would fright the Duchess and the ladies, that they would shriek. And that were enough to hang us all!

All: (Nodding) That would hang us, every mother's son!

Bottom: (Hastily calming down) But I will roar you as gently as any dove. I will roar you, an 'twere any nightingale! *(He chirps some little tiny roars.)*

Quince: (Firmly) You can play no part but Pyramus!

Bottom: (Nobly) Well, I will undertake it.

Quince: (As he passes out the scripts.) Masters, here are your parts. And tomorrow night, meet me in the palace wood, a mile without the town, by moonlight. There we will rehearse.

Bottom: Enough! *(They all shake hands in agreement.)* Hold, or cut bowstrings! *(They leave, going towards the wood.)*

ACT II

(As the announcers speak, two actors change the scenery from Greek pillars to a couple of bushes or trees. A stool or two, covered to look like tree stumps, can complete the scene.)

Announcer 1: So the amateur actors will rehearse in the wood outside of Athens.

Announcer 2: And the runaway lovers will meet in the same wood outside of Athens.

Announcer 1: Unknown to anyone, it is a magic wood, part of Fairyland. And the night they will meet is . . . Midsummer's Eve.

Announcer 2: And on Midsummer's Eve, the elves and goblins and ghosts and fairies . . . walk at night! Here are a couple of them right now!

(The announcers sit as Puck enters from one side and a little dancing fairy from another. The dancing fairy has a basket full of dewdrops—sparkling glitter—that she sprinkles around.)

Puck: How now, spirit! Whither wander you?

Fairy: (Singing or reciting as she dances about.)

Over hill, over dale,
  Thorough bush, thorough brier,
Over park, over pale,
  Thorough flood, thorough fire,

OVER HILL, OVER DALE

music by Sandy Harrison

I do wander everywhere,
Swifter than the moon's sphere.
And I serve the Fairy Queen,
To dew her orbs upon the green.
I must go seek some dewdrops here,
And hang a pearl in every cowslip's ear.

(She stops and points to one side.) Our Queen and all her elves come here anon!

Puck: *(Worried)* The King doth keep his revels here tonight! *(Both spirits look dismayed.)*

Announcer 1: This is not good news, for the King and Queen of Faerie are having a quarrel. Queen Titania has adopted a little boy, the son of a dear friend, and King Oberon wants the child himself for his pageboy.

Puck: Oberon is wrath because that she hath a lovely boy, stolen from an Indian king. And jealous Oberon would have the child knight of his train, to trace the forests wild.

Fairy: *(Looking closely at Puck)* Either I mistake your shape, or else you are that sprite called Robin Goodfellow, "Sweet Puck." Are not you he?

Puck: *(Laughing)* I am that merry wanderer of the night. *(He looks offstage.)* But, room, Fairy! Here comes Oberon!

Fairy: *(Looking the other way in alarm.)* And here my mistress!

(The King and Queen of Fairies enter from opposite sides of the stage. Queen Titania leads the little pageboy they are fighting about. Both rulers have elf and fairy attendants.)

Oberon: (Frowning) Ill-met by moonlight, proud Titania!

Titania: (Frowning back) What, jealous Oberon!

Oberon: (Coaxing) Why should Titania cross her Oberon? I do but beg a little changeling boy.

Titania: (Clasping the child) The Fairy Land buys not the child of me. His mother often gossiped by my side, and sat with me on Neptune's yellow sands. *(Sadly)* But she, being mortal, of that boy did die. And for her sake I will not part with him!

Oberon: (Harshly) Give me that boy!

Titania: Not for thy fairy kingdom! *(To her followers)* Fairies away! *(She and her group fly off, chased by Oberon's elves.)*

Announcer 2: King Oberon plans revenge on Queen Titania.

Oberon: (Calling angrily after Titania.) Well, go thy way. Thou shalt not from this grove till I torment thee for this injury!

Announcer 1: Oberon asks little Puck if he remembers a mermaid singing as she rode on a dolphin's back.

Oberon: My gentle Puck, come hither. *(Puck scurries over to him.)* Thou rememberest once, I heard a mermaid on a dolphin's back, uttering such dulcet and harmonious breath that the rude sea grew civil at her song. And certain stars shot madly from their spheres, to hear the sea maid's music?

Puck: I remember.

Oberon: (Pointing to the sky) That very time I saw, flying between the cold moon and the earth, Cupid all armed. *(Puck looks upward also and nods.)*

Announcer 2: Oberon explains that Cupid tried to shoot his love-arrow at a maiden queen. He missed his target and hit a little flower, which turned purple.

Oberon: A certain aim he took at a fair vestal throned by the west. Yet marked I where the bolt of Cupid fell. It fell upon a little western flower— before, milk-white, now purple with love's wound. And maidens call it "love-in-idleness." Fetch me that flower!

Announcer 1: This flower makes people fall in love.

Oberon: The juice of it on sleeping eyelids laid will make or man or woman madly dote upon the next live creature that it sees! *(Puck grins with mischief.)* Fetch me this herb!

Puck: (Off like a flash to circle the world.) I'll put a girdle round about the earth in forty minutes!

Announcer 2: Oberon plans to make the fairy queen fall in love with something horrible.

Oberon: Having once this juice, I'll watch Titania when she is asleep, and drop the liquor of it in her eyes. The next thing then she looks upon—be it on lion, bear, or wolf, or bull, on meddling monkey or on busy ape—she shall pursue it with the soul of love!

Announcer 1: Then Oberon can steal Titania's pageboy before he breaks the magic flower's spell.

Oberon: And ere I take this charm from off her sight, as I can take it with another herb, I'll make her render up her page to me. *(He hears a noise and looks offstage.)* But who comes here? *(He wraps his cloak about himself.)* I am invisible!

Announncer 2: Into the wood come Demetrius and Helena, hunting the runaway lovers.

Demetrius: I love thee not! *(He looks around angrily.)* Where is Lysander and fair Hermia? *(To Helena)* Hence, get thee gone and follow me no more! Do I not in plainest truth tell you—I do not nor I cannot love you!

Helena: (Crying) And even for that do I love you the more!

Demetrius: I am sick when I do look on thee!

Helena: (Wailing) And I am sick when I look not on you!

Demetrius: I'll run from thee and hide me. *(She hangs on to his hand. He shakes her loose.)* Let me go! *(He runs off.)*

Helena: (Stumbling after him) I'll follow thee! *(She leaves also, weeping loudly.)*

Announcer 1: Oberon plans to help Helena by making Demetrius fall in love with her.

Oberon: (As he lowers his cloak, he calls softly after Helena.) Fare thee well, nymph! Ere he do leave this grove, he shall seek thy love! *(Puck enters.)* Hast thou the flower there?

Puck: Ay, there it is. *(He gives it to his master.)*

Announcer 2: Oberon now tells of a flower garden where Titania often sleeps. He will trick her there with the magic flower. And Puck is to help poor Helena.

Oberon: I know a bank where the wild thyme blows, where oxlips and the nodding violet grows, with sweet musk roses, and with eglantine. There sleeps Titania sometime of the night, lulled in these flowers with dances and delight. And with the juice of this, I'll streak her eyes. *(Puck giggles.)*

(Oberon now gives Puck half the flower and points after Helena and Demetrius.) Take thou some of it. A sweet Athenian lady is in love with a disdainful youth. Anoint **his** eyes. But do it when the next thing he espies may be . . . the lady! *(Puck*

grins with understanding.) Thou shalt know the man by the Athenian garments he hath on.

Puck: Fear not, my lord. Your servant shall do so! *(They leave to find Titania and Demetrius.)*

Announcer 1: Meanwhile, not far away, Titania is ready to go to sleep on her bed of flowers.

(Titania enters with the Indian child. Several little fairies carry a bower, or three branches tied like a tepee, for her to rest in.)

Titania: Come, now, a fairy song. Sing me now asleep. Then to your offices, and let me rest.

Fairy: (Either singing or reciting)

You spotted snakes with double tongue
   Thorny hedgehogs, be not seen.
Newts and blindworms, do no wrong—
   Come not near our Fairy Queen.

Chorus: Philomel, with melody
   Sing in our sweet lullaby.
Lulla, lulla, lullaby, lulla, lulla, lullaby.
      Never harm
      Nor spell nor charm,
   Come our lovely lady nigh.
   So good night, with lullaby.

(Fairies skip off with the child, and Titania goes to sleep in her bower. Oberon tiptoes in and looks about, making sure he is not seen. Then he squeezes the flower into Titania's eyes.)

LULLABY

music by Diane Davidson

You spot-ted snakes with dou-ble tongue,

Thor-ny hedge-hogs, be not seen,

Newts and blind-worms, do no wrong.

Come not near — our fai — ry queen.

Phil - o - mel, with mel — o - dy,
Lul - la, lul - la, lul — la - by,

Sing in our sweet lul — la - by.
Lul - la, lul - la, lul — la - by.

Nev - er harm, nor spell nor charm

come our love - ly la - dy nigh.

So good night with lul - la - by.

Oberon: What thou seest when thou dost wake, do it for thy true-love take! *(He gathers his cloak about him and runs silently off.)*

Announcer 2: And here come the runaway lovers, Hermia and Lysander, who have lost their way.

Lysander: Fair love, you faint with wandering in the wood. *(He looks about.)* And to speak truth, I have forgot our way. We'll rest us, Hermia.

Hermia: Be it so, Lysander. Find you out a bed, for I upon this bank will rest my head. And good night, sweet friend. *(She lies on the ground.)*

Lysander: *(He gives her a kiss on the cheek and moves some distance away.)* Here is my bed. *(The lovers fall asleep instantly.)*

Announcer 1: Puck thinks Lysander is Demetrius, and he puts the magic flower juice on the wrong man's eyes.

Puck: *(Entering)* Through the forest have I gone, but Athenian found I none. *(He looks at Lysander.)* Who is here? This is he, my master said, despised the Athenian maid. *(He sees Hermia and tiptoes to her.)* And here the maiden, sleeping sound on the dank and dirty ground! *(He goes to Lysander and squeezes the flower over his eyes.)* Churl, upon thy eyes I throw all the power this charm doth owe! So awake when I am gone, for I must now to Oberon! *(Puck scampers off, just before Demetrius enters, with Helena running after him.)*

Demetrius: (Pushing her so she falls on the ground.) I charge thee, do not haunt me thus! *(He runs off.)*

Helena: O, wilt thou darkling leave me? Do not so! *(But she is too tired to chase him any more.)* O, I am out of breath. *(She sighs and rises slowly, catching sight of Lysander asleep.)* But who is here? Lysander? On the ground! Dead? Or asleep? I see no blood, no wound. *(She shakes his shoulder, worried.)* Lysander, if you live, good sir, awake!

Lysander: (Opening his eyes and falling instantly in love with Helena.) Transparent Helena! *(He rises, looking for her former lover.)* Where is Demetrius? O, how fit to perish on my sword!

Helena: (With alarm) Lysander, say not so! What though he love your Hermia? Yet Hermia still loves you!

Lysander: No! Not Hermia but Helena I love! *(He kneels at her feet, and she backs away, sure he is making fun of her.)*

Helena: Wherefore this keen mockery? When at your hands did I deserve this scorn? But fare you well! *(She runs off.)*

Lysander: (To his former love) Hermia, sleep thou there, and never come Lysander near. *(Looking after Helena)* And, all my powers, address your love and might to honor **Helen** and to be her knight! *(He runs off after Helena.)*

Hermia: (Awaking from a nightmare, she cries out.) Help me, Lysander! Help me! Do thy best to pluck this crawling serpent from my breast! *(Sitting up, she looks about in relief.)* What a dream was here! *(She holds out a shaking hand.)* Lysander, look how I do quake with fear.

Lysander? *(He does not answer, and she gazes around.)* Lysander! Gone? No sound, no word? *(She grows fearful.)* Alack, where are you? *(There is no answer.)* No? *(She rises, frightened.)* Either death or you I'll find immediately! *(She runs off to find her love, while Titania sleeps on.)*

ACT III

Announcer 2: And here come the amateur actors to rehearse their play. *(Peter Quince and his group of actors enter, not seeing the sleeping Titania.)*

Quince: (As he glances around) And here's a marvelous place for our rehearsal!

Bottom: (Worried) Peter Quince! There are things in this comedy of Pyramus and Thisby that will never please. First, Pyramus must draw a sword to kill himself, which the ladies cannot abide.

Starveling: (Nervously) I believe we must leave the killing out. *(All murmur uneasily.)*

Bottom: (With a good idea) Not a whit! Write me a prologue, and say we will do no harm with our swords, and that Pyramus is not killed indeed.

Quince: (Adjusting his spectacles) Well, we will have such a prologue. *(He makes a note of it.)*

Snout: (Stupidly) Will not the ladies be afeared of the lion?

Bottom: (In a whisper of horror.) Masters, to bring in a **lion** among ladies is a most dreadful thing! For there is not a more fearful wild fowl than your lion living!

Snout: Therefore, another prologue must tell he is not a lion. *(He gives a dumb grin.)*

Quince: Well, it shall be so. *(He makes another note.)* Come, sit down and rehearse your parts. Pyramus, you begin. When you have spoken your speech, enter into that brake. *(He points to a hawthorn bush.)* And so everyone according to his cue.

(They sit and Bottom goes to the center of the stage and poses like a hero. At this moment, Puck peeps out from behind the bush, grinning.)

Puck: What hempen homespuns have we swaggering here, so near the cradle of the Fairy Queen? *(He sees the scripts.)* What, a play toward? I'll be an actor too, perhaps, if I see cause! *(He disappears.)*

Quince: Speak, Pyramus! Thisby, stand forth. *(Flute, who hates to play Thisby, blushes as Bottom drags him forward and kisses his hand.)*

Bottom: My dearest Thisby dear . . . ! *(He cups his hand to his ear and listens.)* But hark, a voice! Stay thou but here, and by and by I will to thee appear. *(He goes behind the bush.)*

Flute: Must I speak now?

Quince: (Nodding) Ay, marry, must you.

Flute: (Taking a deep breath, he shrieks his lines in a high, girlish voice.) Most radiant Pyramus, most lily-white of hue, as true as truest horse, that yet would never tire, I'll meet thee, Pyramus, at Ninny's tomb!

Quince: (Like a director) "Ninus's tomb," man! *(Calls out)* Pyramus, enter! Your cue is past.

Announcer 1: But Puck has put a spell on Bottom!

(From behind the hawthorn come Bottom and Puck, who is dancing with glee. He has put a donkey head on Bottom. However, Bottom does not know it, and he says his lines to Flute.)

Bottom: If I were fair, Thisby, I were only thine!

(For a moment the actors freeze in horror. Then they panic, stumbling around and shouting.)

Quince: O monstrous! O strange! We are haunted. Fly, masters! Help! *(They all run off with Puck chasing them. Bottom scratches his head in wonder.)*

Bottom: Why do they run away? This is to make an ass of me—to fright me. But I will not stir from this place. I will walk up and down here and I will sing. *(He brays out loudly a song about birds.)*

The ousel cock so black of hue,
   With orange-tawny bill,
The throstle with his note so true,
   The wren with little quill. . . .

Announcer 2: Titania awakes, and the magic flower juice does its work.

Titania: (Instantly she falls in love with Bottom, donkey's head and all.) What angel wakes me from my flowery bed? *(Bottom hardly notices her. She puts her arms lovingly around him.)* I pray thee, gentle mortal, sing again. I love thee!

Bottom: Methinks, mistress, you should have little reason for that. *(She kisses him over and over, and he shrugs at her lack of common sense.)* And yet, to say the truth, Reason and Love keep little company together nowadays!

Titania: Thou art as wise as thou art beautiful!

Bottom: Not so, neither. *(Looking about for an escape.)* But if I had wit enough to get out of this wood . . .

Titania: (Holding on to him) Out of this wood do not desire to go. I do love thee. Therefore, go with me. I'll give thee fairies to attend on thee. *(With a shrug he gives in. She pats his muzzle while she daintily calls her attendants.)* Peaseblossom! Cobweb! Moth! And Mustardseed!

Peaseblossom: (Entering with the others) Ready!

Cobweb: And I!

Moth: And I!

Mustardseed: And I!

Titania: (Introducing Bottom like a guest.) Be kind to this gentleman. Feed him with apricocks and dewberries, with purple grapes, green figs and mulberries. The honey bags steal from the humble-bees. And pluck the wings from painted butterflies, to fan the moonbeams from his sleeping eyes. Nod to him, elves, and do him courtesies!

Peaseblossom: (Making a curtsey) Hail, mortal!

Cobweb: Hail!

Moth: Hail!

Mustardseed: Hail! *(Bottom bows to all of them.)*

Titania: Come, wait upon him. Lead him to my bower. *(Bottom goes "Hee-haw!")* Tie up my love's tongue. Bring him silently! *(The Fairies tie up Bottom's muzzle with a rope of flowers and lead him around. At last he snuggles down in her bower, his head in her lap. They sleep.)*

Oberon: (Entering) I wonder if Titania be awaked. *(He looks off.)* Here comes my messenger. *(Puck enters.)* How now, mad spirit!

Puck: (Pointing to the bower) My mistress with a monster is in love! *(He and Oberon laugh.)*

Oberon: This falls out better than I could devise. But hast thou latched the Athenian's eyes with the love juice, as I did bid thee do?

Puck: (He nods vigorously.) I took him sleeping.

Announcer 1: Now the lovers' mixup begins to appear.

(Hermia enters, looking desperately for Lysander. And following her is Demanding Demetrius.)

Oberon: (To Puck, folding him in his magic cloak.) Stand close. This is the same Athenian.

Puck: This is the woman, but not this the man.

Hermia: (Angrily, to Demetrius) If thou hast slain Lysander in his sleep, kill me too.

Demetrius: (Sulkily) I am not guilty of Lysander's blood. Nor is he dead, for aught that I can tell.

Hermia: Never see me more! *(She runs away.)*

Demetrius: There is no following her in this fierce vein. *(He sits down, Oberon sprinkles fairy dust—glitter—on him, and Demetrius falls asleep at once.)*

Oberon: (Scolding Puck) What hast thou done? Thou hast mistaken quite, and laid the love-juice on some true-love's sight. *(Puck bows his head in shame.)* About the wood go swifter than the wind, and Helena of Athens look thou find. See thou bring her here! *(He takes out the magic flower and points toward Demetrius.)* I'll charm his eyes.

Puck: I go, I go—look how I go! Swifter than arrow from the Tartar's bow! *(He whirls off.)*

Announcer 2: Oberon will make Demetrius love Helena.

Oberon: (As he puts flower-juice on Demetrius' eyes.)

Flower of this purple dye,
  When his love he doth espy
Let her shine as gloriously
  As the Venus of the sky!

Puck: (Running in, he points behind him. Helena is being chased by Lysander, who wants a kiss.) Captain of our fairy band, Helena is here at hand.

Puck: Lord, what fools these mortals be!

And the youth, mistook by me, pleading for a "lover's fee." *(He laughs.)* Lord, what fools these mortals be!

Oberon: Stand aside! *(He wraps Puck in the invisible cloak as Helena and Lysander argue loudly.)*

Lysander: Why should you think that I woo in scorn? *(Almost in tears)* Look, when I vow, I weep!

Helena: (Bewildered) These vows are Hermia's.

(Their voices awaken Demetrius. When he sees Helena, magically he falls in love with her.)

Demetrius: O Helen, goddess, nymph, perfect, divine!

Announcer 1: Helena thinks the men are both making fun of her by pretending to be in love.

Helena: (Looking from one man to the other.) O Spite! I see you all are bent to set against me for your merriment. You both are rivals and love Hermia. And now both rivals to mock Helena!

Lysander: You are unkind, Demetrius. For you love Hermia. And here, with all my heart, in Hermia's love I yield you up my part.

Demetrius: Lysander, keep thy Hermia. If I loved her, all that love is gone. My heart to Helen is it returned, there to remain. *(He kneels to Helena.)*

Hermia: (Running in, happy to find her love.) Lysander, why unkindly didst thou leave me? *(She hugs him.)*

Lysander: (Pushing her away) The hate I bear thee made me leave thee so! *(He kneels to Helena also.)*

Hermia: It cannot be! *(She covers her mouth, amazed.)*

Announcer 2: Helena thinks Hermia, her best friend, is making fun of her too.

Helena: Lo, now I perceive they have conjoined, all three, to fashion this false sport of me! *(To her friend)* Injurious Hermia! Most ungrateful maid!

(She speaks of their past together.) O, and is all forgot—all school-days friendship, childhood innocence? We, Hermia, have with our needles created both one flower, sitting on one cushion, both warbling of one song. So we grew together, like to a double cherry. Two lovely berries molded on one stem. Two seeming bodies, but one heart.

(Pleading) And will you join with men in scorning your poor friend? It is not friendly. 'Tis not maidenly!

Hermia: (Bewildered) I am amazed. I scorn you not. It seems that you scorn me.

Helena: (Pointing to the men) Have you not set Lysander to follow me and praise my eyes and face? And made your other love, Demetrius, to call me goddess, nymph, divine and rare?

Lysander: Helen, I love thee! By my life I do!

Demetrius: I say I love thee more than he can do!

Hermia: *(Suddenly in a fury to Helena)* O me! You thief of love! What, have you come by night and stolen my love's heart from him?

Helena: *(Refusing to quarrel, she tries to look tall and dignified.)* Fie, fie! You puppet, you!

Hermia: Puppet! How low am I, thou painted maypole? I am not yet so low but that my nails can reach unto thine eyes. *(She scratches at Helena's face.)*

Helena: *(Backing off)* I pray you, gentlemen, let her not hurt me! She was a vixen when she went to school. And though she be but little, she is fierce! *(The men stand in front of her to protect her from Hermia's claws.)*

Hermia: *(Reaching for her)* Let me come to her!

Lysander: *(Pushing Hermia away)* Get you gone, you dwarf, you bead, you acorn! *(To Demetrius, drawing his sword.)* Now follow, if thou darest, to try whose right is most in Helena!

Demetrius: *(Waving his sword)* Follow? Nay, I'll go with thee! *(The men leave to fight, and Helena starts to run away from her angry little friend.)*

Hermia: *(Standing in her path)* Nay, go not back!

Helena: Your hands than mine are quicker for a fray. My legs are longer, though, to run away. *(She runs into the wood.)*

Hermia: I am amazed and know not what to say.

(Slowly she follows Helena, as Oberon turns to Puck.)

Puck: (Ashamed) Believe me, King of Shadows, I mistook!

Announcer 1: But Oberon will solve it all with a magic fog and a magic cure for the wrong love-spells.

Oberon: Thou see'st these lovers seek a place to fight. *(He hands Puck a stick with a long streamer of gray chiffon on it.)* Therefore, Robin, overcast the night with drooping fog and lead these testy rivals so astray. *(Puck waves the "fog" streamer.)*

Then ... *(Oberon hands Puck another plant, an antidote to the love-juice.)* ... crush this herb into Lysander's eye to take from thence all error with his sight. *(Looking at Titania's bower.)* I'll beg her Indian boy. And then I will her charmed eye release from monster's view, and all things shall be peace! *(He leaves.)*

Puck: (Waving the fog-wand in circles.) Up and down, up and down! Goblin, lead them up and down ... *(He looks off.)* Here comes one!

Lysander: (Entering, he looks as if he cannot see through the "fog" that Puck waves in front of him.) Where art thou, proud Demetrius?

Puck: (Imitating Demetrius) Here, villain! *(Lysander blunders past him and goes offstage, and Demetrius enters, also blinded by the "fog.")*

Demetrius: Lysander, art thou fled? Speak!

Puck: (Imitating Lysander) Thou coward! Come! *(Demetrius chases him around, blinded by "fog" and goes off, as Lysander returns.)*

Lysander: I followed fast, but faster he did fly. *(Puck throws glittering fairy dust at him, and Lysander goes to sleep instantly.)*

Puck: (To Demetrius, who enters, tired out.) Ho, ho, ho! Coward!

Demetrius: (Yawning) Where art thou now? *(Puck throws fairy dust at him, and Demetrius goes to sleep.)*

Helena: (Entering, her heart sick.) O weary night! I may back to Athens by daylight. *(More fairy dust from Puck makes her sleep too.)*

Puck: (Counting the bodies.) Yet but three? Come one more. Two of both kinds makes up four.

Hermia: (Entering sadly) Never so weary, never so in woe. I can no further crawl, no further go. *(The fairy dust makes her go to sleep in mid-yawn.)*

Puck: (While he squeezes the new herb into Lysander's eyes, he chants a poem.)

> I'll apply
> To your eye,
> Gentle lover, remedy.

(He does a wild little dance with his fog-scarf.)

Jack shall have Jill,
   Nought shall go ill,
The man shall have his mare again,
   And all shall be well! *(He scampers off.)*

ACT IV

Announcer 2: Meanwhile, Titania is treating Bottom like a king.

(Titania and Bottom awaken and sit at the "door" of the bower, where she pets him.)

Titania: Come, sit thee down upon this flowery bed, while I stick musk roses in thy sleek smooth head, and kiss thy fair large ears, my gentle joy. *(She puts a rose behind his ear and kisses him.)*

Bottom: *(Contentedly)* Where's Peaseblossom?

Peaseblossom: *(Entering and bowing)* Ready!

Bottom: Scratch my head, Peaseblossom. *(He sighs happily as the elf scratches away. The other fairies enter and help scratch. Bottom strokes his cheeks.)* I must to the barber's, monsieur, for methinks I am marvelous hairy about the face!

Titania: Wilt thou hear some music, my sweet love?

Bottom: *(Nodding happily)* I have a reasonable good ear in music. *(Cobweb inspects one of his ears and makes a face.)*

Titania: Or say, sweet love, what thou desirest to eat.

Bottom: I have a great desire to a bottle of hay. Good hay, sweet hay   *(He starts to hee-haw, and the elves hold their ears. Then Bottom yawns.)* I have an exposition of sleep come upon me!

Titania: Sleep thou, and I will wind thee in my arms. Fairies, be gone! *(The elves leave.)* O, how I love thee! How I dote on thee! *(Bottom begins to snore and Titania kisses him and sleeps too.)*

Announcer 1: And here comes Oberon to break the magic love-spell.

Oberon: (Entering with Puck and the Indian child.) Seest thou this sweet sight? *(He points to the Queen and donkey.)* Now I do begin to pity. And now I have the boy, I will release the Fairy Queen. *(He squeezes the antidote herb on her eyes.)* Now, my Titania, wake you, my sweet Queen!

Titania: (Sitting up, puzzled) My Oberon, what visions have I seen! Methought I was enamored of an ass!

Oberon: (Chuckling) There lies your love! *(He points.)*

Titania: (Backing away from Bottom in horror.) Oh!

Oberon: Robin, take off this head. *(Puck removes the donkey's head from Bottom, who stays asleep. Oberon turns to Titania, as soft music plays.)* Come, my Queen, take hands with me. *(She smiles and takes his hand.)* Now thou and I will, tomorrow midnight, solemnly dance in Duke Theseus' house.

Titania: Come, my lord! *(The fairies fly off.)*

Announcer 2: The Duke and his lady-love arrive in the wood to hunt deer.

(Hunting horns sound. Duke Theseus and Hippolyta enter, followed by Egeus and the court.)

Egeus: (Inspecting the young folk.) My lord, this is my daughter here asleep! And this, Lysander! This, Demetrius is. This Helena. *(He frowns in disapproval.)* I wonder of their being here together!

Theseus: (Mischievously to the lovers, as they awake.) Good morrow, friends. Saint Valentine is past!

Lysander: (Confused) Pardon, my lord. I swear I cannot truly say how I came here. But as I think, I came with Hermia hither. *(The lovers rise and bow.)*

Egeus: (In anger) I beg the law, the law upon his head! *(To Demetrius)* They would have stolen away, they would, Demetrius!

Demetrius: My lord, fair Helen told me of their stealth, and I followed them, fair Helena following me. *(He shakes his head.)* But, my good lord, my love to Hermia melted as the snow. And all the virtue of my heart is only . . . Helena! *(He takes the surprised and happy Helena into his arms.)*

Announcer 1: The Duke over-rules Egeus and announces the lovers can get married in a triple wedding with him and Hippolyta.

Theseus: (To the young folk) Fair lovers, you are fortunately met. *(To the angry father)* Egeus, I will over-bear your will, for in the Temple, by and by with us these couples shall eternally be knit! *(The lovers are delighted.)* Three and three—we'll hold a feast in great solemnity. Come, Hippolyta! *(He leaves with his happy court.)*

Announcer 2: When Bottom wakes up, he thinks he is still rehearsing. *(Bottom slowly stirs.)*

Bottom: When my cue comes, call me. My next is "Most fair Pyramus . . ." *(He looks about, bewildered.)* Heigh-ho, Peter Quince? Flute! Starveling! Stolen hence and left me asleep?

(He blinks his eyes.) I have had a dream . . . *(He pats his body.)* Methought I was . . . *(He feels the top of his head for donkey's ears.)* . . .and methought I had . . . *(He shakes his head in wonder.)*

(Happily) I will get Peter Quince to write a ballad of this dream. It shall be called "Bottom's Dream" because it hath no bottom! And I will sing it before the Duke! *(He leaves hurriedly for Athens.)*

ACT V

(Two actors enter and change the trees for the Greek pillars. To one side they put a bench.)

Announcer 1: The scene now returns to Athens, where all the lovers have been married. Hippolyta and Duke Theseus talk about the lovers' story of enchantment.

Announcer 2: And the Duke tells, in a famous speech, how lovers and crazy people have too much imagination.

Announcer 1: But a poet, through imagination, takes ideas out of the air and makes them into real stories about real places.

Hippolyta: 'Tis strange, my Theseus, that these lovers speak of.

Theseus: More strange than true. I never believe these antique fables nor these fairy toys.

Lovers and madmen have such seething brains! The lunatic, the lover and the poet are of imagination all compact. The poet's eye, in a fine frenzy rolling, doth glance from heaven to earth, from earth to heaven. And as imagination bodies forth the forms of things unknown, the poet's pen turns them to shapes, and gives to airy "nothing" a local habitation and a name. Such tricks have strong imagination!

(He sees the happy couples enter, followed by other ladies and gentlemen.) Here come the lovers, full of joy and mirth. *(After they bow, the Duke calls for his Master of the Revels, who plans the entertainment.)* Come now, what masques, what dances shall we have? Where is our usual manager of mirth? Call Philostrate!

Philostrate: (Coming forward and bowing.) Here, mighty Theseus. *(He hands the Duke a list of acts.)* Make choice of which your Highness will see first.

Announcer 2: It is time for entertainment, including Quince's amateur play, which is really badly done.

Theseus: (Reading) "A tedious brief scene of young Pyramus and his love Thisby, very tragical mirth." *(He looks puzzled.)* Merry and tragical? Tedious and brief? That is, "hot ice"?

Philostrate: A play there is, my lord, some ten words long, but by ten words, my lord, it is too long. My noble lord, it is nothing, nothing.

Theseus: I will hear that play! Go, bring them in. *(Philostrate bows and leaves.)* And take your places, ladies! *(The ladies sit on the bench, and their husbands stand behind them.)*

Philostrate: (Entering and bowing) So please Your Grace, the Prologue is addressed. *(He steps to one side as Quince and his actors enter.)*

Announcer 1: Quince announces a story of famous lovers who had to meet secretly.

Announcer 2: And they came to a tragic end.

Quince: (Bowing) Gentles, perchance you wonder at this show. But wonder on, till truth make all things plain. This man is Pyramus, if you would know. *(Bottom, in armor, bows.)* This beauteous lady Thisby is certain. *(Flute, dressed like a girl with a ribbon in his hair, curtsies, looking very embarrassed.)*

This man doth present Wall. *(Snout, dressed in a box with painted stones, bobs his head.)* And this man, with lantern, dog and bush of thorn, presenteth Moonshine. *(Starveling holds up his lantern.)*

(Quince beckons to Snug, who comes forward in a moth-eaten fur rug.) This grisly beast, which by name Lion hight, the trusty Thisby did affright. All the rest at large discourse, while here they do remain. *(He bows and leaves with Moonshine and Thisby. Wall comes forward, and Pyramus stands to one side, watching him.)*

Wall: In this same interlude it doth befall that I, one Snout by name, present a wall. *(He holds out two fingers spread widely apart.)* And such a wall that had in it a hole or chink, thorough which the lovers, Pyramus and Thisby, did whisper often very secretly. The truth is so!

Theseus: Pyramus draws near the wall. Silence!

Pyramus: *(Booming out in a big, ham-actor's voice, as he looks at the sky.)* O grim-looked night! O night with hue so black! O night, which ever art when day is not! O night, O night! *(He slaps his forehead.)* Alack, alack, alack! I fear my Thisby's promise is forgot!

(He talks to the Wall.) And thou, O Wall, O sweet, O lovely Wall, show me thy chink, to blink through with mine eyne! *(Wall holds out his fingers again.)* Thanks, courteous Wall!

(Wall smiles, and Pyramus stoops to look between the fingers.) But what see I? No Thisby do I see! *(He straightens up and frowns at Wall.)* O wicked Wall! *(Wall looks apologetic.)* Cursed be thy stones for thus deceiving me!

Theseus: The wall, methinks, should curse again.

Bottom: *(He stops acting and goes to the Duke to explain.)* No, in truth, sir, he should not. "Deceiving me" is Thisby's cue. She is to enter now, and I am to spy her through the wall. Yonder she comes!

(Entering, Flute trips over his Thisby skirts and bumps into the Wall. Bottom returns to the other side of the Wall's "crack.")

Thisby: *(In a squeaky voice.)* O Wall, full often hast thou heard my moans, for parting my fair Pyramus and me! My cherry lips have often kissed thy stones.

Pyramus. O kiss me through the hole of this vile
  Wall!

Pyramus: (His hand to his ear, he mixes up his lines.)
I see a voice! Now will I to the chink, to spy an I
can hear my Thisby's face! *(Bending to the crack,
he calls.)* This-by!

Thisby: (Shrieking through the Wall's fingers.) My
love thou art, my love I think!

Pyramus: O kiss me through the hole of this vile
Wall!

Thisby: (After a loud smacking kiss.) I kiss the Wall's
hole, not your lips at all!

Pyramus: Wilt thou at Ninny's tomb meet me
straightway? *(Wall stops to wipe Pyramus's spit off
his hand before he puts it out again.)*

Thisby: 'Tide life, 'tide death, I come without delay!
*(Pyramus strides offstage in one direction and
Thisby in another, awkwardly holding up his
skirts. Wall bows and leaves.)*

Hippolyta: This is the silliest stuff that e'er I heard!

Theseus: (As Lion and Moonshine enter.) Here come
two noble beasts in, a moon and a lion.

Lion: (Very slowly and stupidly) You ladies, you,
whose gentle hearts do fear the smallest monstrous mouse that creeps on floor, may now trem-
ble here when Lion rough doth roar. *(He shows
his face.)* Then know that I, as Snug the joiner, am
no lion.

Theseus: A very gentle beast!

Demetrius: The very best at a beast, my lord, that e'er I saw!

Theseus: Let us listen to the Moon.

(Starveling, playing Moonshine, comes forward with a lantern, a stuffed dog and a thornbush, which were supposed to be in the moon. He tries to explain his moon is a crescent with two horns.)

Moonshine: This lanthorn doth the horned moon present. Myself the Man in the Moon do seem to be.

Theseus: (Interrupting) This is the greatest error of all the rest. The man should be put **into** the lantern. How is it else the Man **in** the Moon?

Demetrius: (Looking at the lantern) He dares not come there for the candle!

(The Moon starts to speak, but Hippolyta interrupts.)

Hippolyta: I am weary of this moon. Would he would change!

(The Moon starts to speak again, but Lysander interrupts.)

Lysander: Proceed, Moon.

Moonshine: (Stammering at the interruptions, he blurts out his speech angrily.) All that I have to say is to tell you that the lanthorn is the moon; I, the Man in the Moon; this thorn bush, my thorn bush; and this dog, my dog. *(He jerks at the dog, which flies up and hits him in the face.)*

Demetrius: Why, all these should be in the lantern, for all these are in the moon. But, silence! Here comes Thisby!

Thisby: (Entering and staring about) This is old Ninny's tomb. Where is my love?

Lion: (Roars) Oh! *(Thisby runs off, dropping her cloak. Everyone applauds loudly.)*

Demetrius: Well roared, Lion!

Theseus: Well run, Thisby!

Hippolyta: Well shone, Moon! *(Moon smiles. The Lion, roaring again, shakes Thisby's cloak in his teeth, spits it out, and exits.)*

Pyramus: (Returning and waving to Moon, who waves back.) Sweet Moon, I thank thee for thy sunny beams! *(Bottom sees Thisby's cloak and stops, shocked as he finds blood on it. He overacts as he recites the poor poetry of the play.)*

What dreadful dole is here!
O dainty duck! O dear!
 Thy mantle good,
 What, stained with blood!

(He shouts in tragical sorrow to the sky.)

Approach, ye Furies fell!
O, Fates, come, come,

Cut thread and thrum!
Quail, crush, conclude and quell!

(He takes out his sword.)

Come, tears, confound.
Out, sword, and wound
The pap of Pyramus. *(He beats at his heart.)*
Ay, that left pap,
Where heart doth hop!

(He stabs himself several times.)

Thus die I, thus, thus, thus . . . *(He lies down, the sword held between his chest and arm. He raises his head to say his last lines.)*

Now am I dead,
Now am I fled.
My soul is in the sky. *(He waves bye-bye.)*
Tongue, lose thy light,
Moon, take thy flight. *(Moon exits.)*
Now . . . *(He dies five different ways.)* . . . die, die, die, die, die. *(He dies at last.)*

Hippolyta: *(Wiping away tears of laughter.)* How chance Moonshine is gone before Thisby comes back?

Theseus: She will find him by starlight.

Lysander: *(As Thisby returns and shrieks.)* She hath spied him already with those sweet eyes!

Thisby: Asleep, my love?

(She thumps Pyramus's head on the floor.)

What, dead, my dove?
O Pyramus, arise!

(She thumps his head several times more.)

Speak, speak. Quite dumb?
Dead, dead? A tomb
Must cover thy sweet eyes!

(She tries to take Pyramus's sword, but Pyramus forgets to release it, so they have a tug-of-war. At last Pyramus lets go, and Thisby stumbles back across the floor. At last she stabs herself.)

Come, blade, my breast imbrue!

(She throws the sword down and blows kisses to the audience.)

And, farewell, friends!
Thus Thisby ends.
Adieu, adieu, adieu!

(With a final screech, she flings herself across the body of Pyramus, who yelps. They die. The audience applauds loudly. Bottom and Flute rise quickly and bow.)

Bottom: Will it please you to see the epilogue or to hear a Bergomask dance?

Theseus: No epilogue I pray you. For your play needs no excuse. *(He motions to Philostrate, who hands Bottom a bag of money. Bottom smiles, bows, and goes offstage with Flute. A clock strikes twelve.)*

The iron tongue of midnight hath told twelve.
Lovers, to bed. 'Tis almost fairy time. I fear we
shall outsleep the coming morn. *(He yawns, and
the others laugh as they parade offstage to music.)*

Announcer 1: As the wedding party leaves, the fairy
folk enter to bless the palace with happiness. *(Instantly Puck scampers in, followed by Oberon, Titania and the Fairies. The music continues.)*

Oberon: Through the house give glimmering light,
Every elf and fairy sprite!

Titania: Hand-in-hand with fairy grace
Will we sing, and bless this place!

*(Here the fairy-folk dance around throwing glitter.
At the end, only Puck is left on stage.)*

Announcer 2: Puck hopes you liked the show!

Puck: (Bowing to the audience)

If we shadows have offended,
Think but this, and all is mended—
That you have but slumbered here.
So, good night unto you all! *(Bowing again)*
Give me your hands, if we be friends,

(He claps his hands to illustrate.)

And Robin shall restore amends!

(He skips off with the last applause. The announcers bow and leave also.)

The End